Sarah Zweig

SM JESSICA BROOKS
DSM 07791 858 157
ASM 07966840.

Popcorn

A play

Ben Elton

Samuel French — London
New York - Toronto - Hollywood

Please see page iv for further copyright information

POPCORN

First presented in association with The West Yorkshire
Playhouse at the Nottingham Playhouse in September,
1996 with the following cast:

Karl Brezner	David Leonard
Bruce Delamitri	Vincenzo Nicoli
Velvet Delamitri	Emily White
Farrah Delamitri	Melee Hutton
Wayne Hudson	Patrick O'Kane
Scout	Dena Davis
Brooke Daniels	Elizabeth Perry
Kirsten	Tamara Letendre
Bill	Bret Jones

Directed by Laurence Boswell
Designed by Neil Irish
Lighting by Jon Linstrum

Subsequently presented by Phil McIntyre at the Apollo
Theatre, London, on 2nd April 1997 with the following
cast:

Karl Brezner	William Armstrong
Bruce Delamitri	Danny Webb
Velvet Delamitri	Paula Bacon
Farrah Delamitri	Debora Weston
Wayne Hudson	Patrick O'Kane
Scout	Dena Davis
Brooke Daniels	Megan Dodds
Kirsten	Sarah Parish
Bill	Richard Laing

Directed by Laurence Boswell
Designed by Jane Clough
Lighting designed by Jon Linstrum

CHARACTERS

Karl Brezner
Bruce Delamitri
Velvet Delamitri
Farrah Delamitri
Wayne Hudson
Scout
Brooke Daniels
Kirsten
Bill

The action of the play occurs principally at the Beverley Hills home of top film director Bruce Delamitri

Time — the present

SYNOPSIS OF SCENES

ACT I
Scene 1 — The day of the Oscar ceremony
Scene 2 — The day of the Oscar ceremony
Scene 3 — The Oscar ceremony
Scene 4 — The night of the Oscar ceremony

ACT II
Scene 1 — The morning after the Oscar ceremony

NOTE

Please note the following contemporary references:

Oprah — Oprah Winfrey — American agony aunt/chat show host
OJ — OJ Simpson — American star acquitted of the murder of his wife in a televized court case
Roseanne — popular TV comedienne

ACT I

SCENE 1

The lounge room of film director Bruce Delamitri's home in Beverley Hills. The day of the Oscar ceremony

The entry to the lounge and staircase to the bedroom are SL. *Two pillars stand each side of the* CS *patio doors overlooking the garden. The doors are covered with drapes and practical shutters which are operated by remote control. An intercom is also visible. There is a large glass coffee table* CS, *an ashtray, telephone, paper and pen, stereo, rug and two sofas with furry cushions. A large drinks cabinet* SL *is filled with bottles, glasses etc. including bourbon and crème de menthe. The back of a TV/video is visible to the audience*

Bruce Delamitri, an extremely famous and equally hip film director in his late thirties, and Karl Brezner, the producer of Bruce's films, have been watching a movie clip on the TV/video. Velvet, Bruce's teenage daughter, sits reading a magazine. As the scene opens Bruce has been watching the clip with Karl. The music ends and as Bruce zaps the TV off with a remote control, the TV is concealed (perhaps electronically)

Karl It's a great scene, Bruce. The clip'll play beautifully.

Bruce I know it's a great scene Karl! I made the damn movie! They're all great scenes, but the scene in the cellar is better. That's the clip they have to use.

Karl They don't have to use any scene, Bruce. They are the Academy and it is their party. Forget the clip, worry about your speech. Did you write it yet?

Bruce I'm not writing any speech, Karl, because I'm not going to win any damn Oscar. I'm too good a director. The Academy is there to celebrate anodyne mediocrity. Anyway it'll be a woman this year.

Karl Well whatever, they are not going to use the cellar clip.

Bruce Why the hell not, what is their problem?

Karl The Chair of the Academy says she feels it's overly gynaecological.

Bruce Gynaecological! Did she watch the movie? The girl's private parts are not shown, they are implied!

Karl Even a subliminal vagina is unacceptable on prime time, Bruce.

Bruce Karl! We do not see her snatch!

Karl Nonetheless, the character Errol stares up it.

Bruce Ironically.

Karl An Oscar telecast is not a medium suited to irony, Bruce. The committee are worried people will just think it's dirty.

Bruce Dirty! How can it be dirty! Errol stares up Conchita's private parts in a manner that clearly implies an ironic juxtaposition, didn't you get that?

Karl Bruce, I just produced the movie, who cares if I get stuff.

Bruce It's so obvious! The very next shot is the private parts' point of view!

Karl Christ Jesus, Bruce, get real. This show goes out to over a billion people the vast majority of whom would be surprised to hear that a vagina can even have a point of view, let alone get it aired on prime time ...

Bruce Of course a vagina can have a point of view! Not intellectually, obviously but cinematically.

Karl Errol's leering mug.

Bruce Yes, except Errol's face is not leering, it's shrugging and that's the point. The character Errol is indifferent. This is all in a day's work for the guy. He's almost — bored! This is just a job. An American job.

Karl Bruce, be realistic! Shooting women in the guts then rummaging about inside them for hidden drugs is not a common occupation.

Bruce Killing is and that's the point I'm making! Being a killer is a career option in America, like teaching or dentistry.

Karl Maybe not quite as common. Bruce, be fair, the Academy are taking a lot of heat here. Yours has to be the most controversial nomination in history. "Ordinary Americans" was about a young couple out on a killing spree and as you are well aware there is currently a very similar young couple on a very similar ...

Bruce Yeah I know, I know! The fucking Mall Murderers. My babies! Every time their crimes are reported the story gets illustrated with a still from my movie! So who's making the association? The psychos themselves? I don't think so. Copy-cat murders for Christ's sake! The lowest, cheapest shot of a hysterical media. Weren't there any sickos around before we had movies?

Karl Society is more violent that it used to be Bruce, that's a fact.

Bruce Exactly, and someone has to get blamed. The politicians won't take the heat! So who gets it? Us, the messengers, the artists. Well, artists don't create society, they reflect it and what's more I'm going to tell them that if I win tonight, which I won't, but if I do and I won't, I will.

Velvet Yeah, and you'll sound like a totally pompous jerk.

Bruce Hey, principles may not mean much to you and your brain-dead pals young lady but I come from the generation that dared to care.

Velvet Please, Dad, I just ate lunch.

Bruce Didn't your mother pick you up yet?

Velvet Yeah, I'm a hologram.

Bruce Your mother is supposed to pick you up.

Velvet Well, I'm so sorry to be still infesting your environment, Dad! Jesus, the stuff I'm going to be telling Oprah one of these days.

Karl Why don't you take Velvet to the Oscars tonight, Bruce? Father and daughter, best pals despite nasty, messy divorce. Nice family image. Respectable. Could play well in the press.

Bruce I don't want to look respectable, I'm a maverick.

Velvet He wants a free hand to pick up some slutlet at the Governor's ball.

Bruce (*to Karl*) Fifteen years old, do you like that?

Karl Generation X, Bruce.

Bruce Generation ex-tremely fucking irritating. I'm working here, Velvet.

Karl If you win an Oscar tonight ——

Bruce Which I won't.

Velvet I think you will.

Bruce Well, I should honey, which is why I won't.

Karl No, but if you do ——

Bruce I won't.

Karl Well, whatever, if you do you have to be nice. Smile, maybe cry a little, whatever, above all don't mention the Mall Murderers. Hollywood does not forgive a party pooper.

Bruce Which is why the intro clip is so important. It's got to have balls.

Karl So now this vagina has balls as well as a point of view, quite some pussy.

Velvet You're disgusting Karl.

Karl Look, they are not going to use the cellar clip; I tried, I failed.

Bruce Well, did you suggest the shoot-out in the bank?

Karl I did, yeah. And they have problems with that too.

Velvet I like that scene, it's cool.

Bruce What kind of problems?

Karl A woman sticking a broken bottle in a guy's dick type problems.

Velvet Great scene, she just totally perforates that rapist asshole.

Bruce Exactly! The female protagonist is clearly depicted in a befittingly empowering light.

Karl After we have seen her befittingly roughed up and taken a long look at her befittingly beautiful tits.

Bruce Her revenge means nothing, unless we see her vulnerability…

Karl *Her tits, Bruce, you can't show tits on network TV!*

Farrah enters. Bruce's nearly divorced wife. A Hollywood survivor in her late thirties

Farrah (*to Velvet*) Hiya baby…

Karl Farrah…

Farrah Oh please Karl. Big night tonight, Bruce. I hope you got a new tuxedo. Remember I cut your Armani into little pieces after I caught you stroking Pussy Woman at the last *Batman* première.

Velvet Cat Woman, Mom.

Farrah I know what I'm saying.

Bruce Noon, Farrah, the deal was noon.

Farrah What? It's such a pain to have your own daughter in the house an extra couple of hours.

Bruce We were supposed to discuss the damn divorce.

Farrah I'll stop by tomorrow.

Bruce What was wrong with today?

Farrah I saw my hypnotherapist. It's an inexact science, Bruce. You can't put deep trauma on hold. When the truth emerges you need to be there.

Velvet Mom's uncovered memories of childhood emotional abuse. She was deprived of attention.

Bruce No, you mean people didn't like her.

Velvet Maybe that's why you and Dad didn't make it, Mom, maybe you're a paranoid dysfunctional incapable of sustaining relationships.

Farrah The reason I can't sustain a relationship with your father, Velvet, is because he is an asshole.

Velvet You used to love him.

Farrah I used to love the Osmonds.

Bruce Hey, if I'm an asshole at least I got that way without any help. Childhood emotional abuse? Jesus, Farrah!

Farrah (*to Velvet*) Can you believe your father? I tell him I've been emotionally abused, what does he do? Emotionally abuse me.

Bruce That's right! We should be celebrating. Farrah just got her self indulgence licence. Now you can drink, you can take drugs, you can fuck up your life completely and none of it will be your fault.

Velvet You two make me want to puke.

Bruce Beautiful, Velvet, I get so proud when you talk that way.

Velvet Well, you raised me, if you can call it that.

Bruce So now I've got bitches in stereo. You hear that, Farrah! So now she's off the hook too, you blame your parents, Velvet blames us, how many generations before the buck stops?

Karl Hey, Bruce, Farrah, you know I hate to break up this …

Farrah Well don't, Karl. I'll go when I want to. This is California, remember. Half this house is mine. (*To Velvet*) Get me a drink, honey.

Velvet Mom you said you weren't going to drink today …

Farrah Hey, give me a break, will you? Can I help it if I have an addictive personality?

Velvet goes to the drinks cabinet and pours Farrah's drink

Bruce You hear that, baby, it's not your mother's fault, her personality's to blame. Nothing is anybody's fault. We're all victims, alcoholics, sexaholics, shopaholics ...

Velvet Hey leave me out of it.

Bruce We are losing more kids a year to violence than we did in the Vietnam war and what are they blaming! My fucking movies!

Velvet hands the drink to Farrah

Farrah Well, surprise surprise, what does he finally get back to? His movies of course. We start off talking about my trauma but in the end we get back to Bruce Delamitri's movies. The only thing on earth that matters. Well the best thing about divorcing you, honey, is that I get not to have to hear about your movies ever again. Forget the drink. (*She puts the glass on the table*) Come on Velvet.

Velvet Good luck tonight Dad. Even if you don't win ——

Bruce Which I won't.

Velvet — and even if you are a pompous jerk ——

Bruce Which I'm not.

Velvet — you're still emotionally relevant to me.

Bruce Thanks, baby.

Farrah Come on, Velvet.

Farrah and Velvet exit

Bruce Velvet's a good kid.

Karl She should be, the money you've spent on her.

Bruce Hey, love has no budget.

Karl Beautiful Bruce.

Bruce OK. So they won't use the cellar clip or the bar room. How about the shoot-out in the bank? That's a nice punchy scene.

Karl Maybe. We can only ask. I'll make the call.

Karl picks up his mobile phone

Black-out

Bruce and Karl disappear

Instantly, through the darkness we hear a screaming shout ...

Wayne (*off*) You are one dead mutha!

SCENE 2

The shout is followed by the sound of gun fire and screams in the darkness. Wayne and Scout appear, carrying machine guns, hysterically elated

Wayne (*shouting*) I love you, sugar pie!

Scout I love you too honey.

Wayne Oh my God, shooting people makes me so horny! I want to do it to you sugar, I want to screw you till your teeth rattle.

Wayne pulls Scout's dress up round her waist

Scout We are in a bank, Wayne! This is a public place! There are people here!

Wayne No problem, baby doll.

Wayne fires his machine gun this way and that, out into the darkness. We hear screams and sobs. Wayne stops firing; the screaming subsides to a few sobs

Scout Oh Wayne, I surely do love you.

Black-out

Wayne and Scout exit. The scene disappears

SCENE 3

On another part of the stage a light comes up. Bruce, wearing a tuxedo, stands at a podium in a single spotlight, an Oscar in his hand

Bruce I stand here on legs of fire — I want to thank you all. Your indomitable spirit has nourished me and helped me to touch the stars. Helped me be better than I had any right to be. Better than the best which is what you all are. Wonderful people. Wonderful Americans, whose extraordinary, awesome, monumental, heaven-sent talent has made me the artist I am. You are the wind beneath my wings — and I flap for you.

God bless you all, God bless America, God bless the world as well.

Thank you.

Huge applause. Bruce disappears. Cut spotlight

SCENE 4

Wayne and Scout appear out of the darkness. Wayne carries a large bag. The Lights begin to fade up

Wayne Ain't nothing like killing, Scout. I done it all in my time, stock cars, broncos, gambling, stealing and I am here to tell you that there ain't nothing to touch the thrill of killing. Yee ha!

The full lights have faded up and we realize that we are in Bruce's lounge room. Clearly this must be a telling moment for the audience as they realize that Wayne and Scout are real and are in Bruce's home. Scout is staring about in child-like wonder

Scout Don't shout so, Wayne. I was just enjoying the early morning peace. Wasn't it a beautiful dawn? Isn't this a beautiful home?

Wayne Sure it's beautiful, sugar pie. The man who owns it is a king in this town. Why I guess he's damn near as famous as we are!

Scout Ain't it something? Don't you just love the furry cushions and glass coffee tables and all?

Wayne You know why they have those glass coffee tables, precious? You want to know why they have them?

Scout So's they can put their coffee down.

Wayne No it ain't, baby. It's so they can get underneath and watch each other take a dump, yes it is honey, I read that, it sure is.

Scout That is not so Wayne! It is just not so and I do not want to hear about it. Just when everything is nice you have to start on about people going to the bathroom on their coffee tables.

Wayne That's the real world honey, it's weird. People are weird, they ain't all nice like you and me. I feel good baby doll, do you feel good?

Scout Yeah, I feel good Wayne.

Wayne I always feel good after I kill a whole bunch of muthas. You know what Dr Kissinger said, baby.

Scout You didn't tell me you'd seen no doctor, honey.

Wayne sits on a sofa and puts his feet up on the cushions

Wayne He wasn't no real doctor, he was the Secretary of State. A powerful man, killed a whole lot more people than you and me ever will and he said power was an aphrodisiac, which means it gets you horny.

Scout I know what an aphrodisiac is, honey.

Wayne Well you ain't never going to get more power over a person than when you kill them so I guess killing is an aphrodisiac too.

Scout I guess so honey — you get your dirty boots off that couch and mind
out for all that blood on your pants. This is a nice house and I'll bet the
people who own it are real nice people and we don't want to get no blood
on their couch.

Wayne They ain't necessarily so nice, pussycat. Besides the blood is dry.
Blood dries real quick on account of it congeals. You know what honey?
If your blood didn't congeal you could die from just one little pin prick.

Scout I know that Wayne.

Wayne And you would be what is known as a homophobic.

Scout Honey, a homophobic is a person who does not approve of carnal
knowledge between a man and a person of the same sex. I believe you're
thinking of a haemophiliac.

Wayne gets up; suddenly he is sullen, sinister

Wayne Is that so?

Scout Yes, honey, it is.

Wayne Is that so?

Scout I believe so, honey.

Wayne grabs her in sudden fury, his fist clenched, ready to strike

Wayne And what d' you call a woman whose mouth is too damn smart, huh?
A woman with a busted fucking lip, that's what.

He pushes her to the ground. Scout screams

Scout No! Please, Wayne, don't!

*Wayne drops to his knees, straddled across her and grabs her throat, fist
raised*

Wayne You think I'm dumb, sugar? Is that it? Huh! Maybe we'd better see
if your blood congeals!

*Scout screams in terror. For a moment it seems that Wayne will beat her.
Instead he kisses her passionately. After a moment, Scout returns the kiss and
embraces him*

Scout Oh, honey, you scared me.

Wayne I know that, cotton candy. I love to scare you because you're just like
a little bird when you're scared.

They are both still on the floor. Wayne is beginning to kiss his way down Scout's body

You like to live in a house like this, cotton candy?
Scout Oh yeah, sure. Like I'm ever going to get the chance.
Wayne We're living in it now, ain't we, honey? I'll bet they've got a real big old bed up them stairs. Stairway to heaven. How about it, cherry pie? How about we go upstairs and make some noise?
Scout I ain't doing no nasty in no strangers' bed Wayne — could be we'd catch AIDS or something.
Wayne You can't catch AIDS offa no sheets ...
Scout If they're dirty sheets, if they're stained.
Wayne Honey plum, these people are millionaires, billionaires even. They ain't going to have no stained sheets. Besides which even if they did you couldn't catch no AIDS off them unless you put them in the liquidizer and injected them directly into your body! Now I bet these people have satin and silk and I do not often get the chance to fuck my little girl on satin and silk.
Scout We do not... (*she checks herself and spells it out*) F-U-C-K, we make love and I don't care if you're coming at me from behind in the rest room of a greasy spoon, it's still making love and if it ain't making love we ain't doing it no more because I do not fuck.
Wayne You're right honey, I stand corrected. And right now I'm just about ready to make love your brains out. So come on honey — let's have us a party. I'll bet they've got a water bed and a mirror on the ceiling and everything — you know something, baby girl? When I get a hold of your ass, I guess I wouldn't let go of it to pick up a hundred dollar bill and a case of cold beer.
Scout Oh Wayne, you know I can't resist your sweet talking.
Wayne Well you don't have to, honey. Get your juicy sex muffins up here.
Scout Don't call it a muffin... (*and improv lines*)

They exit up the stairs. Wayne takes his bag with him

The lights stay up. There is a long pause after which ——

Bruce and Brooke enter. They are still in their evening dress from the Oscar ceremony. Brooke carries a bag, Bruce his Oscar which he places on the coffee table

Bruce I still can't believe my luck. I win an Oscar, and I get to meet Brooke Daniels all on the same night.
Brooke Oh please, Bruce, get real.

Bruce No, I mean it. I'm a fan. I've wanted to meet you ever since I saw the *Playboy* spread, it was wonderful.

Brooke Thanks — again. I don't seem to be able to get away from that. I do acting too, you know.

Bruce (*unconsciously dismissive*). Yeah yeah, you said — so what can I get you? More champagne? The night is young.

Brooke You certainly know how to party, Bruce, it's nearly seven a.m.

Bruce What! Jesus! My wife will be here at ten.

Brooke Your wife? I thought you were divorced.

Bruce Practically. That's why she's coming round, business stuff.

Brooke Oscar at night, alimony in the morning, life in the Hollywood fast lane.

Bruce She enjoys making my life uncomfortable.

Brooke Oh well — I guess we still have a couple of hours …

There is a significant pause

Bruce I wasn't planning on going to bed — to sleep I mean.

Brooke Nice table.

Bruce I like it.

Brooke I can think of a good use for it.

Bruce Help yourself.

Brooke takes some cocaine out of her bag and begins to chop it up on the table, on which now stands the famous statuette

Brooke Just to keep you bright and cheery for your wife. First time I ever did drugs with Oscar looking on; I hope he doesn't disapprove.

Bruce Hey, who cares if he does, that little eunuch is mine now. I own him.

Brooke You sure do. (*She snorts a big line of cocaine*)

Bruce OK, so we're partying! (*He closes the shutters and turns the stereo on*) I'll get some glasses.

Brooke You know the one thing I didn't like about "Ordinary Americans"?

Bruce What?

Brooke The sex scene.

Bruce What are you, a nun? That was the sexiest scene I ever made. I edited it with a permanent hard-on.

Brooke Sure it was sexy — but it wasn't true, everything else in the movie was so real. The guns, the attitude, the blood all over everything — why couldn't the sex be real too? The only place over-acting is still encouraged is in sex scenes. Did you ever see *Nine and a Half Weeks*? Jesus you only had to tap that woman on the shoulder and she had an orgasm. Why can't the sex be convincing? Convincing is sexy. Girls wear pantihose, you

know, not stockings, when they get laid they have to take off their
pantihose. I never saw a girl take off pantihose in a movie.
Bruce That, I'm afraid, is because pantihose is not sexy. It is impossible to
remove pantihose in a sexy manner.
Brooke You think so?
Bruce I know so, it cannot be done.

Brooke snorts up the last of the lines and stares at Bruce for a moment. She
stands before him and begins to dance

Brooke You want to bet?
Bruce What are the stakes?
Brooke I'll tell you if I win.

The music plays

Brooke's hands are on her thighs now, massaging the material of her dress,
working it up her legs. She contrives to collect the folds of the dress about her
hips in a bouquet-like cluster, almost as if she is wearing a rather flamboyant
tutu. In one quick movement, almost a jerk, Brooke pulls the handfuls of cloth
right up high, pulling the folds of skirt to just under her breasts revealing all
of her pantihose and some of her bare midriff besides. Her hose is of course
of exquisite quality. High-waisted, covering Brooke's whole stomach, ending
a few inches below her ribs in a wide, black, delicately-embroidered
waistband. Brooke's whole lower body is now on show, from diaphragm
down to the stilettos she wears. All encased in sheer black nylon. Above it all
she holds her dress in great silky folds. Bruce is very impressed so far

She hooks her thumbs under the waistband of her hose and pulls the material
slightly away from her skin. Whilst still contriving to hold up her dress she
begins slowly to pull the hose downwards, until her arms are fully extended.
She raises one leg and places her foot on the glass table. The hose which is
now pulled down to a few inches below the gusset of her knickers stretches
out taut between her thighs, lending the tiniest suggestion of bondage and
constraint to her sultry pose

Bruce leans forward and undoes her shoe. Brooke brings her leg back to the
ground and with equal balance and elegance raises the other one. Bruce
undoes the shoe. Brooke kicks off her shoes and stands for a moment on the
rug, holding her dress above the half-descended top of her pantihose

In one movement she lowers herself to the floor whilst simultaneously pulling
the tights down to her knees. She rolls backwards on to her back, whilst

*bringing her knees up to her chest. Lying on her back and keeping her knees
close to her chest, she rolls the tights right down to her ankles and along her
feet until they cover only her toes which point seductively at Bruce. One final
push on the tights and they fall down. She raises herself, picks up the tights,
and gets to her feet. She steps towards Bruce and drops the pantihose into his
lap. She switches off the music*

So?

Bruce So I hope you don't expect me to be that good with my socks. You
win. What were the stakes?

Brooke Come here.

They embrace, but Brooke breaks away

Just let me get some protection.

Bruce You know what, I think I love you.

*Bruce frantically undresses. Brooke reaches down to her bag which is by her
feet. Suddenly Brooke produces a gun from her bag and swings round and
pushes it into Bruce's face*

Brooke Touch me you bastard and I'll blow your brains out!

Bruce What the fuck is going on!

Brooke You think just because I've done nude modelling I'm some kind of
whore!

Bruce No, I ——

Brooke You looked at me and you saw sex, right? From the first second I've
just been a piece of meat as far as you're concerned. Well, now you're
going to pay!

Bruce Listen Brooke, this is not necessary ——

Brooke Get on your knees and kiss my feet!

Bruce What!

Brooke You heard. Kiss my feet!

*Brooke is levelling the gun at Bruce; he is terrified. He drops to his knees on
the floor and tentatively kisses her feet*

I said kiss them don't wipe your nose on them.

Terrified, Bruce kisses with more vigour

Bruce Look — Brooke, I'm sorry — clearly I misunderstood the situation
— now if I've offended ——

Brooke Are you scared?
Bruce Yes I'm scared.
Brooke How scared?
Bruce Very fucking — What do you want?
Brooke I — want — a part in your next movie. (*She lowers the gun*)

It takes a moment for Bruce to realize what's happened

Bruce What …?
Brooke I'm an actress, I want a part — that was the stake.
Bruce Put away your gun.

Brooke puts the gun back in her handbag

(*Furiously*) You mad crazy fucking bitch!

Brooke quickly argues her point

Brooke Your movies make people horny and scared. What did I just do to
you! Come on, be honest!
Bruce Pamela Anderson makes me horny, Saddam Hussein makes me
scared. I'm not going to put either of them in my movie — you made me
kiss your feet! At gun point! I ought to call the cops!
Brooke I've sent you fifty letters! Fifty! Did you see them? Did you read
them!
Bruce Have you any idea how many actresses and models write to me! I
don't see any of that stuff. I have people.
Brooke I guessed you didn't, that's why I decided to do what I did.
Bruce Have you been planning this all along?
Brooke Yes.
Bruce You're fucking insane. I ought to call the cops.
Brooke I made you horny and I made you scared — be fair, I did; you've
got to give me a chance.
Bruce Supposing I said it depended on you sleeping with me?
Brooke (*after a pause*) No. I don't screw on a professional basis.

Again a pause

Bruce Pity — OK, I'll give you a screen test, you crazy bitch. Have your
agent call me next week. Believe me, there is no chance that I will forget
you.
Brooke Thank you, Bruce, thank you very much. I promise I won't
disappoint you.

Bruce You can't disappoint me any more than you already did.

Brooke Hey, I said I didn't screw on a professional basis. I already got my screen test.

After a pause they embrace. Within moments the pent-up frustration bursts and they are writhing together on the couch

> *They are too absorbed to notice Wayne enter, carrying his machine gun and bag. Wayne crosses to the sofa. Brooke has had her face buried in Bruce's neck, she comes out and sees Wayne. Obviously she is pretty freaked*

Bruce — Bruce — for Christ's sake Bruce, behind you!

Bruce looks behind him, sees Wayne and falls off the sofa in fear, trying to pull up his trousers as he does so

Wayne Morning folks.

Bruce Who are you? — Brooke, do you know this guy? Is this part of your joke thing?

Brooke I do not know this man, Bruce.

There is a very tense stand-off. Wayne stares at Bruce, then walks over to him while still covering Brooke with his gun. He stares hard at Bruce, putting his face right up close

Wayne I don't believe this. I do not be-fucking-lieve this. I'm actually here, I'm actually meeting Bruce Delamitri. I can't tell you what a pleasure it is to meet you sir. I've been planning this a long time. Scout! C'mon in here and say "Hi". Oh yes, this is a real thrill, sir. This is awesome. Scout, get your dumb ass in here right now!

> *Scout enters rather sheepishly. She is, like Wayne, heavily armed*

Scout Hi.

But Bruce and Brooke can only stare in reply

> We messed up your sheets some — but you know, with modern detergents there shouldn't be any problem.

Wayne It don't matter about no sheets, sugar. We can buy more sheets. This is Bruce Delamitri. You are looking at the man here. The man. I told you we'd get to meet him, baby, and here we are.

Wayne gestures at Bruce. He is holding a machine gun so it is rather alarming

Scout How d'you do, Mr Delamitri. Wayne's a real big fan of your pictures, sir, he's seen them dozens of times — me too, I like them too but Wayne, he loves them.
Wayne But I guess you get real tired of people telling you all that stuff.

There is a pause. Wayne and Scout are acting like embarrassed fans, except that they are so heavily armed

Bruce Do you want money? I have money, about two thousand dollars in cash, and there's some jewellery...
Wayne Mr Delamitri — may I call you Bruce? We don't want no money. We got money, we got more money than we can spend and we don't spend nothing anyway because we steal all our stuff. We just came around to visit with you. Is that OK? How about we sit down? Maybe we could have us a drink? Would that be OK? I like Bourbon and Scout here'll take anything sweet.

Bruce gets the drinks. The others sit, there is a nervous tension. Obviously Bruce and Brooke are pretty scared. Scout turns to Brooke in an effort to make polite conversation

Scout You're Brooke Daniels, aren't you? Yes, you are, I'd know you anytime from all the magazines you've been in — *Vogue* and *Esquire* and *Vanity Fair* — I love all that stuff it's so glamorous and nice — I've been in a magazine too...
Wayne Sure Scout, "America's Most Wanted".
Scout It's a magazine! Isn't it, Brooke? — Brooke? It's a magazine isn't it? "America's Most Wanted" is a magazine, isn't it?
Brooke Yes, it's a magazine.

Bruce gives Wayne his drink

Bruce Look — if you don't want cash I have a customized Lamborghini parked right outside that...
Wayne Bruce, I just told you we're here to visit. I don't want your damn car. I got a car. An American fucking car, made with sweat and steel, not some wop faggot-built pile of tin shit. A Lamborghini! Bruce I am surprised at you. When you drive a foreign car you are driving over American jobs.

Bruce backs off, scared. He gives Scout her drink

Bruce This is *crème de menthe*.

Scout I love cocktails.

Wayne (*turning to Brooke*) Why'd you do that *Playboy* spread, Brooke? I
mean I ain't saying it wasn't beautiful because it was but hell I would never
let Scout do a thing like that.

Scout Oh, c'mon Wayne, as if anyone would ever want to see me in *Playboy*
magazine!

Wayne Sure they would honey, excepting I wouldn't let you do it on account
of the fact that my rule is that if a man looks at you with lust in his eyes, I
kill him. So if you was to be in *Playboy* I'd just about have to kill half the
men in the United States.

Scout You're getting there anyway, honey!

Wayne Scout's exaggerating, Bruce. So why'd you do it, Brooke?

*Brooke is too scared to answer. Scout knows the answer, she had read it in
a magazine*

Scout She did it, Wayne, because being an in-control woman does not mean
denying one's sensuality. Isn't that what you said, Brooke? I read that. She
didn't do it for men, Wayne. She did it for herself because she is beautiful
and there is nothing wrong in celebrating that. It's called Girl Power.

*But Brooke is still not up to replying, she can only nod, there is another pause.
Again it is down to Wayne and Scout to keep the conversation going*

Wayne Well I guess that makes me feel a whole lot better about jerking off
in the john over it, Brooke. I confess I never realized I was doing such a fine
and empowering thing…

Scout Wayne!

Wayne I want to ask Brooke something now, Scout, and I don't want you
getting mad at me. OK?

Scout Well it depends on what you ask her, Wayne.

Wayne What I want to ask is how'd those girls in *Playboy* magazine get their
hair the way they do? It always looks so damn perfect.

Brooke finally finds a voice

Brooke Well — you know, I guess it's just a question of hairdressing really.
They use a lot of mousse and they back light it and sometimes they put in
extensions…

Wayne Brooke, I do not mean that kind of hair.

Scout Wayne!

Wayne Well I want to know! I mean we tried shaving it, sugar, and you just
ended up like some kind of damn Mohican with a rash!

Scout turns to Brooke, mortified with embarrassment

But in *Playboy* magazine those girls just have a little tuft like that was all
that ever grew. It don't look shaved or nothing. These are adult women!
Not little girls, but all they got's a little tuft. How'd they do that?
Brooke Well, Wayne — one has a stylist.
Wayne (*hugely amused*) A stylist! A pussy hair stylist! Now that would be
one hell of an occupation. Yes sir, I guess I could get to like that kind of
work.
Scout Wayne, that is enough!
Wayne (*delighted with his comic thought*) Yes sir! I'd work weekends and
all the overtime the boss'd give me. I'd be saying "Can I shampoo that for
you madam?" I'd work hard and get me my own salon — there'd be a
whole row of women sitting reading magazines with little hair dryers on
…! (*He cries with laughter*)

Scout is furious

Scout That is enough, Wayne!

Bruce has found some courage. He picks up an intercom phone

Bruce OK, now I've buzzed down to my security guard. He's in the lodge
at the gate. If you leave now, he won't hurt you but if you harm us, he'll
kill you.
Wayne *He'll* kill me? Well ho, fuckn' ho. (*He cocks his gun at Bruce*)

Bruce stands frozen, holding the intercom phone

Bang — Just kidding you, Bruce. You give that guard a call. If it makes you
feel better you give that old boy a call.

Scout, still mortified over Wayne's comments, turns to Brooke

Scout Brooke, I am so sorry that Wayne has gotten to prying into your
personal stuff. He does not understand that a woman likes to keep her
special private places special and private.

Wayne is watching Bruce on the phone. Bruce is clearly getting no reply

Wayne He ain't answering you, Mr Delamitri. Maybe he can't hear you
…Here, let's see if we can't get his ear a little closer to the phone.

*Wayne takes a knife from his belt and reaches into his bag. He clearly cuts
something and then produces a severed ear. Brooke screams, Bruce is
equally horrified. Wayne carries the gory ear over to Bruce, takes the
intercom phone and holds it to the ear*

(*Shouting*) Hallo! Hallo! Mr Security Guard! — He don't hear so good
does he. (*He holds the ear up to his own lips and shouts at it*) Hey! You hear
me! The guy who pays your wages is calling you, you fucking jerk! (*To
Bruce*) How much did you pay the guy, Mr Delamitri? Was he expensive?
Because if he was you are being ripped off, Bruce. He wasn't worth shit
as a guard. He just sat there in his hut with his big dog and we crept up
behind him and killed him.

Scout We didn't kill the dog.

Wayne That's what's wrong with this country! People just don't do the damn
jobs they're paid for. No wonder we can't get ahead of the Japs. (*He
casually drops the ear into the ash tray*)

Bruce Listen, I don't know who you are but…

Wayne Just no count white trash Bruce. We ain't nothing. The only
memorable thing I ever did in my life was killing people.

Scout (*proudly*) We're the Mall Murderers. I'm Scout and this is Wayne.
We're the Mall Murderers.

Wayne Scout, I tell people that — we're the Mall Murderers.

Brooke Oh God, are you going to kill us?

Wayne Now what kind of question is that? Me and Scout here never know
who we're going to kill till we done it.

Scout It just happens. This is so great isn't it? — I mean us all here together,
just sitting talking. Because like, Bruce here is Wayne's hero and I've
always admired girls like you Brooke, so beautiful and all. 'Cept I can't
deny I think it's a shame about all this cosmetic surgery you girls get done.
Cause these days you don't know who's really beautiful and who's just a
cut-up sucked-out balloon-boobed bitch.

Wayne So what we all going to talk about now?

After an embarrassed pause, Bruce has a go

Bruce Well uhm — why don't you tell us something about yourself,
Wayne…

Wayne Now why the hell would a famous man like you want to know about
any of my stuff, Bruce?

Bruce Well — I guess, to be frank, from what I know of your — uhm, work,

it seems to me that you kill people whom you do not know. — So, I suppose
I thought it might be kind of nice to — get to know you.

Wayne Well, OK Bruce. What can I tell you?

Bruce Well — how about you tell me what it's like to kill someone.

Wayne You want to kill someone? Hell man, do it, it's easy, do it.

*Wayne takes his pistol from his belt and opens the chamber, he removes all
but one bullet from the drum and offers the weapon to Bruce*

Five, four, three, two, and one left for you. Here take it. Come on. One bullet
can do a lot of damage.

Bruce grabs the gun and points it at Wayne

That's right, you could kill me, or Scout here, 'cepting of course if you did,
vengeance would not be a long time a'comin' — well Bruce, you going to
kill someone?

*There is a pause while Bruce decides whether to kill Wayne or not. Bruce puts
the gun down*

Bruce I don't want to kill anyone, Wayne. I just wanted to know what it's
like.

Wayne Well, hell, man, you might as well say what's it like to make a movie.
It depends, on the circumstances, on the victim. I'll tell you what it ain't
like, it ain't witty.

Bruce Witty?

Wayne Yeah, like in "Ordinary Americans", when Mr Chop Chop and the
other guy get the guy's hand and stick it in the food processor. You
remember that scene?

*Wayne takes Bruce's hand and mimes the food processor scene from the
movie*

Bruce Yes, I do.

Wayne It whizzed up blood and chopped onions and stuff all over their suits
and the one guy looks at the other and says, "Shit, this suit's Italian". It got
a big laugh. But we knew they have to go to this real swanky hotel to waste
this dude, there ain't no way they're gonna get into no real swanky hotel
with all blood and chopped onions all over 'em. So they have to go to the
launderette and strip off to their shorts and sit with their big guns on their
laps reading women's magazines…

Scout That's my favourite bit when they talk about hormone replacement therapy...

Wayne But they don't know how to work the machines, so when they get to the real swanky hotel to waste the dude, their suits is all tiny like a little kid's suit, 'cause they shrunk. Man, that was one classy scene.

Bruce Thank you.

Scout I don't know how many times Wayne watched that movie.

Wayne They said it was ironic and subversive in the *New York Times*; I just thought it was a classic, the way they kept on wasting people.

A buzzer sounds

Now who's that coming calling? You ain't pushed no alarm button or nothing have you, Bruce? I'd kill you inside of two seconds.

The buzzer goes again

Bruce I think it's my wife, my ex — we have a settlement to discuss — she's very erratic about time keeping.

Scout Farrah Delamitri! My God I would love to meet her. Didn't I read somewhere you wished she was dead?

Bruce I was quoted out of context.

The buzzer goes again

So I leave it, right?

Wayne You've made an appointment, you keep it. I guess she can see your big old Italian Lambor-fucking-homosexual parked out in the drive and I don't want her getting suspicious about nothing.

A buzzer goes again

Bruce Look, surely we don't need to drag my wife into this. I mean ——

Wayne Ain't going to drag nobody into nothing, Bruce, you just have her come on up here, do your business like you would anyhow and then she can go.

A buzzer goes again. Bruce picks up the intercom

Bruce Hallo? ... Karl! What the Hell are you...? Listen Karl, it's the morning after the Oscars for Christ's sake...

Wayne Who is it, Bruce?

Bruce It's my producer, he's ——

Wayne Tell him you're sending someone down.

Bruce is about to protest but Scout points the gun at his head

Bruce OK Karl, I'll get someone to let you in.

Wayne puts the guns away in his bag. He also takes Scout's bullet belt. Scout is left with her handgun

Wayne I'm going to take a nice stroll down to the gate and let Karl in so we can visit with him for a while. Now he don't have to see no guns or nothing but Scout and me are going to be ready and anybody who tries to mess around with us is going to be one dead mutha, you hear? Now you just sit tight till I get back. Scout, honey, you're in charge.

Wayne exits

Scout Sit down, Mr Delamitri. I don't want to have to kill you but I will.

Bruce sits on the floor. Again there is an uncomfortable pause. Brooke, terrified but strong, starts to try and get through to Scout

Brooke You know Scout, I think I saw that picture of you. The one in "America's Most Wanted". I remember — I remember it was pretty amazing. You're very photogenic.
Scout Yeah?
Brooke Sure, you're a pretty girl, you know that? Real pretty.
Scout (*coyly*) Oh, I don't think so.
Brooke Of course you are Scout, and I think you know it too. Except you don't make as much of yourself as you could. Like for instance you have beautiful hair, but you haven't done anything with it.
Scout Well, all blood and bits of brain and stuff got in it when Wayne pumped this guy who was serving me a soda so I had to rinse it through and now it's a mess.
Brooke Well, I could help you with that Scout. Maybe we could do some make up. I bet you'd look like a movie star. Don't you think so, Bruce?
Bruce Yes, Scout is very pretty.
Brooke I bet any agent would love to have a cute little girl like you to work with.
Scout Why would they notice me? I mean I ain't saying I ain't pretty. Wayne says I could have any man I wanted, 'cepting only for as long as it took him to shoot the guy. But there's a heap of pretty girls in this town.
Brooke OK Scout, I'll be straight, you're a celebrity. You're a killer's girl...

Scout I'm a killer too.

Brooke Well, sure, but the world is going to know that he made you do it and in the meantime if I make you as pretty as can be...

Scout You really think I could be a star? — You mean you'd help me?

Brooke Of course I'd help you Scout, I like you. We could be friends.

Scout That's easy for you to say while Wayne's threatening to kill you.

Brooke Maybe so, but it seems to me that Wayne is always going to be threatening to kill someone so how are you ever going to make any friends?

Scout I don't know. Sometimes I wonder about that.

Brooke Listen to me, Scout. If ever a person needed friends it's you. We could help you, but you have to help us. Don't you want friends?

Scout Sure I want friends.

Wayne enters with Karl

Wayne Bruce, this here's Karl.

Karl Hi Bruce, having a party?

Bruce Yeah, kind of. This is Brooke Daniels...

Karl Brooke Daniels. Well well well. Miss February, I didn't recognize you with your clothes on. That was a great spread by the way.

Brooke Thank you.

Karl I'll bet the nozzle of that gas pump was cold, am I right?

Wayne laughs

Who're these two, Bruce, or will the answer make me blush?

Bruce A couple of — actors. I saw them in an improv' night out at Malibu — thought I'd talk to them. Might be right for "Killer Angels".

Karl Seeing actors on the morning after Oscar night? That is dedication. No offence to you guys, but for me talking to actors is only one step away from slamming my dick in a door.

Bruce I just thought they had, you know, maybe they had the right look.

Karl For "Killer Angels"?

Bruce Maybe.

Karl Well, I'm just the schmuck who finds the money, but these kids look about as much like psychopaths as Scooby Doo.

Wayne Would you like me to fix a drink, Mr Brezner?

Karl Water.

Wayne Water? — Well OK, Scout, go get a glass from the bathroom.

Karl Not tap water! Christ Jesus! When I drink water there has to have been at least twenty thousand feet of Alpine granite between me and the last person who pissed it. Get me an Evian.

Bruce I don't have any Evian. Karl, what do you want?

Karl Maybe we could talk down by the pool.

Wayne coughs uneasily

Bruce We'll talk here. I am busy.

Karl Well, excuse me. I forgot for one moment that you just won an Oscar and therefore are professionally obliged to treat with contempt those whom formerly you have loved and respected.

Bruce Karl, I didn't sleep either. Could we do this another time?

Karl Maybe you didn't see the papers today.

Bruce No I didn't see the papers.

Karl Well, I hate to be the shit delivery boy here, but as predicted, yours is not a popular Oscar choice. Frankly the editorials would be kinder if they'd given it retrospectively to "Attack of The Ninety-Foot Booby Woman".

Bruce Who gives a fuck what those parasites think?

Karl We give a fuck, Bruce. It's the violence thing. The *issue du jour*. Newt Gingrich was on the "Today Show" this morning, he says you're a pornographer and you should not get honoured for glamorizing murderers.

Bruce Can we do this another time, Karl?

Karl *Another time*! If being called a murderer by the entire right wing of American politics doesn't worry you perhaps would like to recall that we are severely *financially* exposed here…

Scout is bored with this conversation

Scout Brooke, will you put my hair up like you said you would?

Brooke Uhm yeah, sure, OK…

Rather nervously Brooke takes her handbag and goes over to start doing Scout's hair. Karl is a little disconcerted but carries on

Karl Clearly the Republicans want to make a mid-term election issue out of it. They think they've got a live one and we need to make a plan.

Scout You know what I love, I love the way mousse comes out of the can. How do they get it all in there?

Wayne It expands, honey.

Scout I know it expands, dummy, because it's bigger when it gets out! But I don't know how it happens, it's the same with cans of whipped cream. How do they *do* that! I mean cream is cream, you can't crush it up.

Karl is astonished at these rough-looking people who are so confidently ignoring him

Karl Excuse me, did I become invisible? I'm talking here.

Scout Sorry.

Karl Well, you are very far from welcome. We can kiss goodbye to a fifteen
on the video release. That's half our rental gone to say nothing of actual
bans, particularly in the South. This damn Oscar could kill us. Can you
believe that?

Bruce Yeah, sounds bad Karl, let me think about it a while...

Karl still can't believe a man as powerful as he is being interrupted

Karl It's these fucking Mall Murderers, Bruce. Christ, what kind of pointless
sickos are those people.

Bruce (*quickly*) Well you know — I mean, you have to try and see things
from their point of view.

Karl What, you mean the point of view of a socially inadequate jerk-off?

Brooke is still nervously working on Scout's hair

Brooke I really don't think that you can dismiss them that easily.

Karl Pardon me, miss, for appearing rude, but that I should give a fuck what
you think. Wayne Hudson and that weird, scrawny little bitch he drags
around are fucked-up trailer-park white trash nobodies who have mashed
potato instead of brains. The sooner they get fried, the better. I would gladly
take them out myself.

There is a pause. Bruce and Brooke are terrified at this outburst

Bruce (*laughing*) Ha ha. Nice speech. You talk big Karl, but you'd never do
it, you always end up on the side of the underdog.

Karl Underdog? Those scum? Like I would waste my tears on such maggots.
I would piss on their graves and that of their mothers who no doubt were
whores.

Wayne You think the Mall Murderers are fucked-up white trash, Mr
Brezner?

Bruce He does not think that...

Brooke You can't just dismiss them...

Scout (*to herself*) Weird, scrawny little bitch?

Bruce He did not mean that! You should hear the way he talks about his wife.

Karl Excuse me! What is this right now? Oprah? Are we having some kind
of debate about these filth? Of course they're fucked-up trash.

Bruce Karl! What do you want! I'm busy here, I have stuff to do and you are
getting in my face.

Karl What do *I* want! What do you think I want! Look you have to fight this,

it won't go away. Get out there today and work the chat shows. Tell the
world that these killers are not your responsibility and ——

Wayne OK Bruce. I'm sick of this guy now. We have things to talk about.

Bruce Karl, I appreciate you coming round and I'm going to think over what
you said, but right now I'm busy OK so ...

Karl (*astonished*) You want me to go?

Bruce Yes I do.

Karl Because you have stuff to do with these people?

Bruce Yes.

Karl looks at Wayne and Scout with distaste. He turns discreetly to Bruce

Karl Look Bruce, if you want something rough to mess around with you
should talk to me. We're in enough trouble. This is dangerous, you're
going to end up blackmailed.

Bruce Karl. Go.

Karl is mystified and offended

Karl OK, see you.

Wayne See you.

Wayne takes out his gun and shoots Karl dead

Bruce (*shouting*) No!

Brooke, who is doing Scout's hair, screams, and pulls the hair

Scout Ow! You pulled my hair!

Brooke (*nearly hysterical*) I'm sorry!

The buzzer goes

Pause. Black-out and another buzzer

ACT II

The action is continuous from Act I. Karl is dead on the floor. The buzzer is buzzing

Wayne Answer it.
Bruce It's going to be Farrah. My wife.
Wayne Answer it.
Bruce I'm not bringing her into this.
Wayne So tell her to go away. But make it good: if she kicks 'n' hollers, you all cross Jordan together.

Bruce stares at the corpse of Karl

Bruce Why? — Why did you kill him?
Wayne He called my best girl a weird, scrawny little bitch, Bruce. What would you have done? What would Mr Chop Chop have done?
Bruce (*shouting in anger*) I would not have killed him and nor would Mr Chop Chop who is a fictitious character that I invented, you insane bastard!
Wayne I know that Mr Chop Chop is a fictitious character, Bruce. That don't mean he don't exist now does it? You gon' tell me Mickey Mouse don't exist? Maybe you think old Walt's been counting make-believe money all'a these years. Maybe you paid for this house with green stamps.
Bruce Mickey Mouse, like Mr Chop Chop is a — is a — I'm not talking about Mickey Mouse! My friend is dead!
Wayne Because he dissed my baby so stop working yourself up into ten types of asshole and answer the damn door!

Bruce speaks into the intercom

Bruce Farrah, I can't see you right now.... I have a woman here, Farrah! I'm partying! Go away!... Well I do care.... No! Farrah! Don't... Don't!... (*He puts the phone down*) She has a key, she's coming in.
Wayne Well, I'd better move old Karl here then. You don't want to be having no discussion about who gets to keep the wedding presents over a dead body.

Wayne starts to drag the body out of the room

Bruce And you'll let her go when we're done?

Wayne Maybe. Long as she don't call us no names. Sit down Bruce, relax, make yourself comfortable, you want things to look normal for your wife, huh? Scout, you keep these good folk on a tight lead, you hear?

Scout Okey dokey smokey.

Wayne drags Karl out

I'm sorry I shouted at you Brooke. I didn't mean nothing, it's just you pulled my hair.

Brooke Scout. Listen to me. This can't go on. Sooner rather than later you're going to get caught and the more trouble you cause the worse it's going to be.

Scout We know that Brooke. But Wayne's got a plan. That's why we came here.

Brooke What plan can he possibly have?

Scout I dunno but he's got one. "I got me a plan hon", he says "and everything is go'n be just fine." That's what he said. He has a plan for our salvation.

Bruce His plan is to get you both killed.

Brooke Bruce, would you mind? Scout and I are talking here.

Bruce (*ignoring Brooke*) That's how it's going to happen, Scout; the cops will come, Wayne'll fight and you'll both be shot to ribbons.

Scout Well, if that's how it is then it's OK with me, Mr Delamitri. We'll go out together, in a hail of blood, love and glory. Love and glory. Me 'n' Wayne are going get that tattooed on us one day. It's our motto.

Brooke Love and glory. That's beautiful, Scout, really beautiful. Love and glory — and you do love him don't you, Scout? You love him very much.

Scout I love him more than my life. If I could pull down a star from the sky and give it him I would. If I had a diamond the size of a TV I'd lay it at his feet. I got feelings, Brooke, bigger than the ocean, deeper than the grave.

Brooke Wayne needs help, Scout, and if you love him you'll make sure he gets it. Let us be your friend, Scout, let us be his friend.

Scout If they take him they'll put him in the chair. They'll melt his eyeballs when he ain't even dead yet. That's what the chair does t'ya. I read it.

Brooke Maybe it doesn't have to be that way, Scout. Maybe if we bring him in peacefully they'll put him in a hospital. Bruce is a big man in this state, Scout, he can help — let us be your friend, Scout, let us be his. Give me the gun, Scout.

Scout is wistful, she almost seems to be day-dreaming

Scout You think I should give you my gun?

Brooke It's best for us all, including Wayne.

Scout If I give it to you, will you be my friend?
Brooke I said I would be didn't I, Scout, and I keep my word. Give me the
   gun.
Scout OK.

Scout smashes Brooke in the face with the butt of her gun. Brooke falls back,
bleeding at the mouth

   (*Shouting*) I sure fucking gave it to you didn't I, you bitch! You my friend
   now? You always keep your word, don't you! So now you're my friend!
   Say it!

Brooke, lying bleeding, struggles to reply

Brooke I'm your friend.
Scout Well, I don't want you for my friend, you whore, because you tried
   to turn me against my man and that is unforgivable! — Maybe you want
   him for yourself! Is that it? Are you coming on to my Wayne? If you try
   it, bitch, I'll cut you into pieces! Now sit down, you slut, and wipe your
   mouth. We got company coming.
Bruce Yes, that's right — Wayne said to look normal — normal.

Brooke staggers, sits down and dabs at her bloodied mouth. Scout sits down
and puts a cushion on her gun. Bruce sits very stiffly. It is all very stiff and
contrived

Scout Maybe we should be talking about something — uhm — you know
   what I heard? The Martians got Elvis. Uh huh. But that ain't the spooky
   part. The truth is, they took him in '68 and replaced him with a blob — of
   ectoplasm — in a jump suit.

   Wayne enters ushering in Farrah and Velvet. He has concealed his gun.
   For the moment there are no guns visible, although what with Brooke in
   an evening gown hiding a bleeding lip plus Wayne and Scout's trashy
   appearance, and the stiff poses, the scene still looks pretty weird

Wayne Bruce, your wife's here.
Farrah Some party, Bruce. Socializing never was your strong point was it?
Velvet Didn't you sleep yet, Dad? You are so gross.
Bruce Velvet! What the hell are you doing here? This is between me and your
   mom.
Velvet Well I'm so sorry to visit my own father the day after he wins an
   Oscar. I mean obviously you'd far rather party — with — who are these
   people Daddy?

Bruce Uhm — well, they're friends of mine, this is Brooke Daniels and——

Farrah Brooke Daniels? Oh pur-lease! *Playboy* bunnies, Bruce? That is so tacky.

Brooke I was never a bunny, bitch. I was a centrefold. And actually, I'm an actress.

Farrah notices Brooke is bleeding

Farrah Well either way, sweetie, if this is some kind of "S and M" thing and he's been beating up on you, you make your claim out of his share of our property, not mine.

Suddenly Bruce grabs Velvet and pushes her to the door

Bruce Get out, Velvet. Right now, get out. I don't want to see you.

Velvet Please, Daddy, don't try and order me around, it's embarrassing. I'm a grown woman now. I have made an exercise video.

Bruce What the hell did you bring her here for! Farrah. Go now! Get her out!

Farrah I brought her here, Bruce, to remind you that she and I are two and you are one and that should be reflected in the settlement.

Velvet is viewing the assembled group slightly nervous

Velvet Yes, Daddy and this stuff is private — and it's morning. I mean can't these people just go now?

Wayne Oh there ain't nothing private between me an' your ol' man, precious. We're his friends, I'm Wayne and this is Scout by the way.

Farrah Velvet's right, Bruce, your "friends" should go now. Just give them their money and...

Bruce My friends are staying Farrah, I told you I'm busy! So get Velvet out of here! Now!

Farrah Bruce what's got into you? You are speaking about your own daughter! You disgust me, you'd rather be with sluts and street trash than——

Bruce No Farrah! You don't mean that...

Scout wanders into the conversation

Scout Mrs Delamitri?

Farrah looks and turns to her with haughty distaste

Farrah Excuse me?

Scout Is it true you got so puke drunk one time you miscarried? That you
    retched up so hard you done lost your little baby?
Farrah What did you say?
Scout Well that's what it said in the *National Inquirer*.
Farrah How *dare* you speak to me in that manner! What is going on here
    Bruce? Is this some kind of dumb divorce tactic? Are you trying to throw
    me? Because it won't work.
Bruce Please, Farrah, get Velvet out of here. You can have what you want,
    everything, I swear. Just take Velvet away now!

Farrah finally realizes something is wrong

Farrah Are you all right, Bruce?

Wayne laughs. Suddenly Farrah and Velvet are very worried

Velvet Mom, I think we should do this later.
Farrah I'll have my lawyer call, Bruce. Come on, Velvet, we're outta here.

Farrah makes to leave. But Wayne gets up

Wayne No need for them legal parasites to get involved, Mrs Delamitri.
    Fuckin' lawyers are eating away at the soul of this country. So fuck 'em I
    say. Fact is, I'll be handling Mr Delamitri's side of the negotiations from
    now on. Is that OK with you?
Farrah Come on, Velvet, we'll talk to your father another time.
Wayne Truth is, Mrs Delamitri, Bruce here wants you dead. I heard him say
    so himself and I have decided in view of all the pleasure your husband has
    given me in the past, to fulfil his wish.

Wayne produces his gun

Bruce For God's sake, Wayne, let them go! You said you'd let them go.
Farrah Bruce! What is going on!
Velvet Daddy, do something!
Wayne You said you wanted her dead, he said that, didn't he, Scout?
Scout I heard it.
Farrah Bruce — are you trying to have me *killed*?
Wayne You don't go saying stuff you don't mean, do you, Bruce?
Bruce It was a figure of speech, Wayne! For God's sake, man, it was a figure
    of speech.
Farrah Whatever he's offered, I'll double it!

Wayne Bruce, it is not such a big deal. People get killed every few seconds, In South Central LA they're pleased if they make it through lunch. If your balls drop you're a survivor, you're an old man! C'mon, let me waste the bitch, I'll take the rap and you get to keep everything.

Wayne raises his gun. Velvet screams. Bruce is desperately trying to talk Wayne down

Bruce Look, Wayne, I said I wanted Farrah dead because I was imagining something that in thought might be nice but in reality is obnoxious. Like have you ever said "I could eat a horse." I'll bet you've said something similar now of course you don't actually *want* ——

Wayne Are you patronizing me, Bruce?

Bruce No…

Wayne You think I don't know the difference between a figure of speech like "I could eat a horse" and a man who's telling the truth even though he's too gutless to admit it. You hate this bitch, if she'd died in her car coming here today you'd have been dancing a jig.

Scout Sure he would.

Wayne If fate was to take this fossilized Barbie-looking bag of bones out of your life that would be just fine. Well I'm fate. The bitch has met a psycho killer. Ain't your fault, so don't fight it. Watch me drop her and count your blessings.

Wayne raises his gun. Velvet screams

Bruce Don't! Please don't! I don't want her dead, all right! I don't care what I may or may not have said in the past, I'm telling you now, I don't want her to die! And if my opinion means anything to you, which you keep saying it does, I'm begging you, don't kill her. Just leave her alone. Please!

Wayne lowers his gun

Wayne OK OK, just trying to do you a favour, no need to get mad.

Unnoticed, Brooke has been edging towards her bag. Now while attention is centred on Bruce she slips out the gun that she had tricked Bruce with in Act I and jams it against the back of Scout's head

Brooke Drop your gun right now, Wayne, you sadistic bastard or I'll blow this sick little bitch's brains clean across the room!

There is a pause. Wayne is genuinely surprised at the development

Wayne Don't you go pointing no gun on my baby now.

It is a stand-off. Wayne has swung round and is pointing his gun at Brooke; she is pointing hers into Scout's head

Scout She won't do it, Wayne.
Brooke Oh yeah? I want to kill you so bad, Scout, I can taste it.
Wayne You know, Brooke, if you kill Scout the rest of you will be dead inside of one heartbeat.
Brooke Maybe so, but you love her and you don't love us. Her for us ain't no trade. So drop your gun right now or I drop her!
Wayne Well, I guess what we have here is a Mexican stand-off. You know the thing I always think, when you get these kind of situations in movies. When two guys are pointing pieces at each other and sweating and all, like there's some problem. I always think why doesn't one of them just quit talking and shoot.

He fires; Brooke falls down, shot

I mean that has to be the sensible thing to do, doesn't it?

Velvet screams. General shock

Bruce My God, Wayne! How long is this going to go on?
Wayne Well, it can't go on much longer can it, Bruce?
Bruce Velvet, get some napkins from the drinks cabinet, to stop the blood.

As Velvet gets the napkins, Bruce gets a cushion and makes her comfortable

She's got to have a doctor.
Wayne No can do Bruce. Ain't no doctor in my plan.
Farrah What? What plan? Who are you? What is going on?

We hear the beginnings of the sound of a helicopter

Wayne The plan for mine and Scout's salvation. I guess they should be here by now.
Bruce Who should be here?
Wayne The rest, Bruce, I know you're a mighty important man in this town but even you can't save us on your own.
Bruce Who can? Who is coming to save you?

The helicopter noise is getting louder

Wayne Why the cops and the TV cameras and the reporters and the people
   of America, who else? — Sure ain't gonna be no Seventh Cavalry; this ain't
   the movies, Bruce.
Scout TV cameras! Oh Wayne, I surely do love you…

*Scout rushes up to the patio doors. The noise of the helicopter is getting
louder. Scout pulls back the drapes. Some kind of lighting effect should occur,
ideally light should stream through the glass patio doors, silhouetting the
actors as the audience blink in the glare. It is, however, morning, so perhaps
a combination of sun light and flashing cameras*

*Scout excitedly looks out the windows and the helicopter noise crescendos;
the lighting should tell us that it is flying past. As the chopper noise fades we
hear a chorus of shouts of "Scout", "Scout — over here" and a hundred
motorized camera shutters. Then a police megaphone: "Wayne Hudson.
Wayne Hudson. We know you are in there…"*

   (*Exhilarated, shouting*) Wayne, there's hundreds of them!
Wayne I know that, baby doll, now let's close those doors, huh! We ain't
   ready yet.

*Wayne aims the remote at the shutters and they close. The reporters, voices
become muffled*

Bruce Ready for what?
Scout They are making some mess of your lawn, Mr Delamitri. I sure hope
   you're covered for this type of eventuality.
Bruce Is this a hostage thing, Wayne? Are we your shield?
Wayne I don't hide behind no woman, Bruce. Where's your damn TV?

*Bruce reveals the TV screen. Wayne laughs. Wayne puts the TV on. We hear
the sound of news reporters as Wayne switches channels*

Reporter's voice on TV — standing outside the house of Oscar-winning
   director Bruce Delamitri where it is believed that ——
TV voice — notorious mass murderer Wayne Hudson and his young partner
   Scout ——
Another TV channel — appear to have taken refuge at the home of the
   renowned film maker who is said to have inspired their killing rampage…

Bruce can't believe what he's hearing

Bruce Jesus, they're blaming me.
Wayne I sure hope so, man.

Wayne switches the TV channel again

Another TV channel Mr Delamitri, last seen leaving the Oscar ceremony
   in the company of nude model Brooke Daniels ——
Brooke I am a fucking actress!
Wayne Keep it down Brooke, I'm watching TV here.
Another TV voice — leaving a trail of pillage, mayhem and death,
   murdering indiscriminately in the manner of the fictitious anti-heros of
   Bruce Delamitri's Oscar-winning movie "Ordinary Americans"...

Bruce is stunned

Bruce They're blaming me! Jesus Christ, they are blaming my movies!
Farrah You hear that, Velvet, now he's angry, someone's dissing his
   movies. Never mind I nearly got shot by the Mall Murderers!
Velvet Mom! Brooke did get shot!
Wayne Well, I guess if you're just going to keep on talking we might as well
   have the damn TV off.

Wayne turns off the TV

Scout I was watching that, Wayne. How come you always get to hold the
   thing.
Farrah Wayne, you have to let us go, if the cops are here you can't escape
   and ——
Wayne I don't want to escape, Mrs Delamitri. I asked them to come here.
   I called them.
Bruce You called the cops?
Wayne No, I called CBS, they must have called the cops, but that don't
   matter none. Me and Scout here are used to ignoring cops.

The phone rings. Wayne picks it up

   Guess this'll be them. (*Into the phone*) Yeah. ... That's right, this is Wayne
   Hudson. Mm mm, besides Bruce Delamitri we got Brooke Daniels who is
   an actress by the way and we got Farrah Delamitiri who is a Gucci-wrapped
   sad sack of silicone and Scotch and their daughter Velvet, cute as a button,
   good TV if I have to.... No you listen to me.... Just give me a number right
   now where we can talk to you.... OK thank you, we'll be back in a little
   while...

Having taken down the number he leaves the phone off the hook

Bruce What are you doing, Wayne?
Velvet Good TV if you have to what? What do you mean?
Bruce What is your plan?
Wayne Well, I guess a plan to avoid being executed for murder, Bruce. I mean that has to be a priority for me and Scout right now.

Brooke gasps from the floor where Velvet is trying to treat her

Brooke You won't get away. You're going to fry, you bastards.
Velvet This woman needs a doctor.
Wayne Soon, maybe. You got to understand here, Miss Delamitri, that I don't mind none if people get dead.
Bruce What is your plan, Wayne, for Christ's sake?
Wayne Well, Bruce let me tell you. As you know, Scout here and me have committed murder and mayhem across four states. Now I wish that I could tell you that every one of those corpses deserved to get shot. I wish I could say it was like the movies where rapists, red necks, bad cops, hypocrites and child abusers get what they deserve but it just ain't so.
Scout They might have been all those things, Wayne. We never knew any of them long enough to find out.
Wayne Well whatever, honey. The point I'm making here is that we are in deep shit. We are going to get caught damn soon now and when we do, like Brooke here has pointed out, we have a higher than average chance of getting fried in the chair. And that, Bruce, is where you come in.
Bruce What do you mean?
Scout Wayne says you're our saviour.
Farrah Give them what they want, Bruce, anything, just give it them!
Velvet Yes, give it to them, Daddy!
Bruce I don't know what they want! Tell me, I'll give it to you whatever it is.
Wayne We want an excuse, Bruce. We want someone to take the blame.
Bruce Someone to blame? What the hell do you mean someone to take the blame? Some kind of magician? Like the whole thing was an optical illusion and someone else shot all those people?

Brooke coughs in a deathly manner

Velvet She needs a doctor! You can't just let her ——
Farrah Velvet ——
Wayne Listen! I did not ask that bitch to threaten my baby! She is in this dire

situation by her own choosing, so shut the fuck up because me and Bruce
are talking here.

Velvet But, I just think ——

Wayne Or maybe I should shut you up for good?

Farrah Not the nose, it's new!

Velvet begins to cry

Wayne All of you, I said shut the fuck up!!

Wayne raises his fist ready to strike Velvet

Bruce Hurt her and I swear whatever you want from me you will never get!!

Wayne rounds on Bruce

Wayne You'll do exactly what I tell you to do whether I break this bitch's
pretty little face or not.

Velvet (*sobbing in fear*) Don't hurt me!

Scout Now, there's no need to go beating up on no little girls, Wayne, it's
beneath you.

Wayne This ain't no little girl, precious pie! Kids're born old in Hollywood.
Why this little slut must'a spent more money already in her few short years
than your sweet momma would'a earned in fifty lifetimes. She deserves a
punch in the mouth!

Bruce You'll get nothing from me if you hurt her!

Wayne lowers his fist

Wayne I want you to know, Bruce, that I am minding the wishes of my baby
here and not you. Because I can assure you that you will do whatever I tell
you to do whether I hurt your little girl or not.

Bruce (*desperate now*) And what is it! *What is it you want me to do*?

Wayne I want you to plead on our behalf. I want you to speak up for us and
save us from the chair.

Bruce Plead on your behalf. You're crazier than I thought. You think my
word's going to save you from the punishment you deserve? You're guilty
as Hitler.

Farrah Just do it, Bruce! Why do you always have to know better?

Wayne Sure we're guilty if by that you mean that we done all the stuff they
say we done, but that ain't the point is it? Not these days? These days no
matter how guilty you are, you can still be innocent.

Bruce No, from my limited knowledge of jurisprudence I don't think so.

Wayne Yes. From my extensive knowledge of trial by TV I know so. For
instance like that chick who cut off that guy's dick right? She was guilty
all right, she never denied it. She cut off that ol' boy's manhood and threw
it out of a car window. Do you see that bitch in prison? Huh? Is she breaking
rocks in the hot sun? No, because although she was guilty, she was
innocent.

Scout That's right: she done it, but she was innocent and I agree with her.
That bastard beat up on her and he done raped her too. I hope she used a
rusty knife.

Wayne Now, Scout, you know that you and me disagree on this issue.
Personally I don't see as how no woman can get raped by her husband on
account of the fact that he is only taking what's his anyway.

Scout He is such a dinosaur.

Wayne Personally I think that any Mexican bitch who cuts the dick off an
ex-United States Marine who has served his country, should rot in a hole.

Scout The court agreed with her.

Wayne The court was a bunch of lesbians and faggots — anyway, whatever,
we're getting off the point here. What I'm saying is, right or wrong, the
greaseball bitch walked free. She done it, she said she done it, she was glad
she done it, but she walked. Guilty but innocent you see. You can be both
in the land of the free, always assuming that is that you got an excuse.

Bruce But you've just said yourself you didn't even know your victims, that
they were blameless. Are you suggesting that there is any excuse for mass
murder?

Wayne Bruce, there is an excuse for anything and everything in the USA!
What about them cops who beat up on the black boy and started a damn
riot? They was videoed! You see them doing time? No sir, you do not.
Remember OJ? They said he killed his wife. Turned out they'd got the
wrong victim. The dead chick wasn't the victim at all. No way, OJ was the
victim. He was the victim of a racist cop, who incidentally also walked.
Nobody gets blamed for anything in this country, *nothing is anybody's
fault*. So why the hell should we take the rap for what we done, huh?

Wayne picks up the phone and dials

Velvet Daddy, there's nothing to discuss! Just say what he wants you to say!
Farrah Listen to your daughter, Bruce.
Bruce I'm thinking here!
Wayne (*into the phone*) OK. We gon' make a statement y'hear? We gon'
announce our intentions and tell it like it is, so what we want is a small ENG
crew hooked up to all the stations. Cable too. We ain't giving no exclusive
here. Also they got to have a direct line to the ratings computer. I want to
know just how big a TV star I am minute by minute. Now I give you my

word as a freeborn American that the TV people get safe passage, I
guarantee they will not be harmed on account of you are observers, man,
we are the action.

Scout ENG. That means Electronic News Gathering. Ain't Wayne smart?

Wayne (*into the phone*) Now I know what you're thinking, guys. You're
thinking 'bout putting a SWAT team in here. Bunch of damn commandos
dressed up as TV people right? Well forget it, the crew you send me best
be the smallest crew there is. I am talking one operator and one recordist.
What is more they have to come in barefoot and wearing only their
underwear. Y'hear me? And I ain't talking no baggy long johns or old
ladies bloomers here. I am talking the kind of jocks you couldn't hide a nail
file in.

Farrah Velvet, straighten yourself up and don't get blood on your jacket,
there's going to be cameras.

Wayne (*still into the phone*) Uh huh — Now I'm going to come down and
check every inch of the people you send and if you fuck with me cop, four
more innocent people going to get very dead real soon and it will be *your
fault;* what is more every TV station in America's gon' see it. Bye bye now.
(*He puts the phone down*) OK now, we'd best prepare our statement.

Bruce I'm not making any statement with you!

Scout Are we really going on the TV, honey?

Wayne Yes we are, baby doll, and so's Bruce here because if he doesn't——

Farrah No Wayne.

Wayne I may just kill his darling daughter.

Bruce We can't address the fucking nation!

Wayne Oh yes we can, Bruce. You are going to announce to the whole of
the USA, and believe me it will be because between you and us we got more
celebrity than Elvis making out with OJ using Roseanne for a mattress.
You are going to tell the whole USA that we are your fault.

Bruce You're insane.

Wayne You are going to say that having met us and talked to us you realize
that we are just poor, dumb white trash and you and your glamorous
Hollywood pictures done corrupted our po' simple minds...

*Wayne takes up the bag which contains the severed head and pulls out a
bundle of blood stained magazines and newspapers and starts to hand them
to Bruce*

You're going to say you admit that your work is — what's it say there
Bruce, I highlighted some stuff with Scout's magic marker...

Scout I love stationery.

Bruce Wayne, you can't seriously believe that...

Wayne What's it say, Bruce?

Bruce (*reluctantly reading*) "Delamitri's work is wicked, cynical exploitation and manipulation of the lowest basest elements of the human psyche. His Oscar nomination is an insult to the dead and bereaved of America." It won't work Wayne! These columnists are cynical reactionaries pursuing a transparent anti-liberal agenda!

Farrah Jesus, Bruce, enough of this bullshit please, it isn't the time.

Wayne It will work Bruce because you are going to tell the world that me 'n' Scout are weak-willed, simple-minded creatures who have been — what's it say in the *Tribune* there Bruce, just read it out would you——?

Bruce "— seduced by Hollywood's pornographic imagery of sex and death."

Wayne Images *you* create, man! And for which you have just been honoured with an Oscar. You are going to say that your eyes have been opened and you are *ashamed*.

Scout And so you should be by the sound of it.

Wayne In fact, I got an idea, man! Oh yeah! You're going to return your Oscar.

Bruce My Oscar?!

Wayne That's right, you're going to give it back on live TV. Out of respect for your victims. The people *you* killed *through* me and Scout.

Bruce It won't work, Wayne! It can't. Whatever I say or do won't change the law.

Wayne Bullshit, Bruce, and you know it! The law is whatever people want it to be! It ain't never the same thing twice. It's one thing to a white man, another to a black. One thing to the rich and another to the poor. The law is a piece of fuck'n' Play Dough, no-one knows what shape it's going to be in next. Man, after you've made your broadcast me, and Scout here, won't be no punk killers no more. We'll be hundred things, we'll be heroes to some, victims to others, we'll be monsters, we'll be saints. We will be the defining fuck'n' image of a national debate! A debate that'll go to the core of our society.

Scout Don't you just love it when he talks like that? I don't know where he gets all that stuff.

Wayne TV, honey. A man can pick up a lot of fancy-sounding bullshit if he watches TV all his life.

Bruce Wayne, listen to yourself, defining fucking image, for Christ's sake! Who do you think you are. You're a punk, a dirty little punk.

Velvet Daddy, be nice!

Wayne Come on, man! It doesn't get any better than this. The King of Hollywood, two mass murderers, a dying *Playboy* centrefold, a rinsed out hag of an ex-wife, a spoilt, sexy little weeping teen — blood, guns — we've got it all. Nobody will ever forget this, it will be burned on their minds forever, and every time anyone sees you, Bruce, they'll remember you with

your arms round me and Scout, Brooke dying at your feet saying:
"America, wake up! We sow a wind and we reap a whirlwind."

The phone rings

Honey! Get the phone.
Scout (*into the phone*) Hallo. ...My name is Scout, how may I help you?
Wayne (*grabbing the phone*) You got the crew?
Scout (*to Velvet*) That's how they take calls in motels, I think it's nice. All
Wayne ever says is "yeah".
Wayne Yeah. I'm coming down, OK, Bruce, you just start thinking about
what I told you because I guess you know what I'll do if you don't, that is
if'n Scout hasn't done it already. See you in five, baby.
Scout I'll be here waiting for you, hunk.

They embrace and Wayne exits

They all sit. Scout's guns are much in evidence

Ain't Wayne smart, huh?
Bruce Not if he thinks I'm going to do this thing for him, he isn't smart at
all.
Scout Oh you'll do it. You ain't boss here any more.
Bruce You think I'm going to buy into this circus! This media feeding
frenzy! I won't. I can't. There is such a thing as creative integrity, you
know.

With a supreme effort Brooke speaks up

Brooke I have been shot!
Velvet Don't talk Brooke, it puts pressure on your wound.
Brooke He's worrying about his fucking image.
Bruce Hey Brooke, I didn't shoot you and I have stuff to think about here
too! I know you're hurt bad and when I can do something to help you I will.
Right now however, I am powerless...
Velvet You don't have to go on about your creative integrity though, Dad.
I mean it's kind of gross.
Bruce I'm thinking about the social implications of this thing. What they are
asking is immoral, it's obscene. — They want me to make excuses for
murder. — Already people pass the buck for just about everything, from
drink driving to ——
Farrah Jesus! Back with that. Can't you change the record, Bruce.
Bruce I will not be a party to the further immoralization of America!

Farrah Bruce, you're such an asshole.

Velvet Immoralization is not a word.

Farrah No wonder the Democrats never invite you to their conventions no matter how much money you give them.

Bruce This man wants me to confess to mass murder on television! I can't do it!

Scout Yes, you can, asshole.

Velvet Dad. Listen to yourself. He's shot Brooke. He said I'd be good TV if he did whatever, nobody cares that you don't like it. You have to say it that's all.

Bruce And when I do, I'm dead.

Brooke Ha!

Bruce Well, not actually dead, but dead both morally and as an artist. Listen baby, I won't let him hurt you, I've got to think this through. That bastard doesn't just want to destroy what I am, but what I've been! Everything I've done and achieved. He wants me to say my whole life has been a piece of pornography.

Farrah So what? Who cares?

Bruce So what? So fucking what! My life work, Farrah! My legacy, belittled and soured. That scumbag, that shit!

Scout You'd better watch your mouth.

Bruce What? You want me to like the guy, Scout? Your boyfriend is a sadistic maniac, a heartless psychopath.

Scout You don't know his nice side.

Bruce I have a duty as a public figure here!

Farrah Hey Bruce, here's an idea, how about you shut your dumb mouth for a minute, huh?

Bruce What?

Farrah We're all tired of your bullshit and there are practical considerations here.

Bruce Practical considerations, what, more practical than my life?

Brooke Ha!

Farrah Listen — Miss — Scout? I'd like to ask you a favour — would it be all right if my husband made a call? Or maybe sent a fax.

Scout It depends...

Bruce What the hell's on your mind, Farrah?

Farrah Bruce, think about it. So what if this thing ruins you as an artist? Who gives a fuck. It's time you got a life anyway. The real point is it will completely destroy you financially.

Velvet Mom!

Farrah Once you claim responsibility for inciting murder, the families of every victim of violence in America are going to sue the living ass off you.

The criminals too come to think of it! What we have to do right now is transfer your assets and property into my name. If Miss Scout here will let you make a call…

Velvet Mom! For God's sake!

Farrah Lady I am protecting your future.

Scout You're quite something aren't you?

Farrah I just don't happen to want some Milwaukee waitress whose husband got knifed in a bar getting hold of my money.

Scout Well he ain't gonna make no call. So I guess you'll just have to think about being poor.

Farrah Poor, oh my God.

Scout Personally I reckon maybe that waitress in Milwaukee would have a point. Maybe your damn high and mighty moral husband shouldn't have made the films he did.

Bruce What did you say?

Scout Well you know, films and TV, they used to be an escape from being poor and living in fear, now they just rub your nose in it.

Bruce Well don't go then, you can watch *The Waltons* on cable.

Velvet Daddy don't be so patronizing.

Scout I mean you live in a big old house in Hollywood and you pay for it by making films that show real people, people who live in ghettos and trailer parks, look ugly and sick and violent…

Bruce You are ugly and sick and violent!

Farrah Bruce!

Bruce Well…

Scout I know I am, I know that, and I deserve whatever I get … It just seems to me that half of America is living in hell for the entertainment of the other half.

Wayne enters, accompanied by Bill and Kirsten who are a small camera crew, in their underwear. Obviously they are very nervous. They carry a camera, camera stand, boom microphone, ratings monitor, headphones, radios etc.

Wayne OK everybody we're getting somewhere here. It's media city out there Bruce — The Wayne and Scout Village! We got every damn network 'cept the Home Shopping channel and I guess they may not be long.

Scout I love that shopping channel. The way they can just keep on talking about a little bracelet or a nutmeg grinder.

Wayne Honey, not now.

Scout I mean, sometimes, you didn't even know you wanted a musical vegetable shredder.

Wayne Honey, *not now*. This is Bill and Kirsten, they are going to send our message to the nation — I sincerely apologize for the working conditions — OK Bruce you're the director. Where should these people stick their camera?...

Bruce is now angry and confused enough to be reckless

Bruce You know where you can stick it, Wayne.
Velvet Daddy for Christ's sake!
Bruce He isn't going to shoot me Velvet, he needs me.
Velvet He doesn't need me!
Wayne That's true enough, young lady, you tell your daddy.
Bruce I've told you you'll get nothing from me if you hurt her.
Wayne Well anyways, I guess I can do this myself. Maybe I'll get an Oscar too ha ha! — OK, I reckon you guys can set up down there — well come on we haven't got all day, chop chop, ha — Chop Chop.

Bill and Kirsten set up DSC *with their backs to the audience*

OK now, I think I got my visual concept together here — you like that Scout, visual concept?
Scout You know I love it honey.
Wayne If we see this area here as kind of centre of the action — Scout move that coffee table.
Scout I ain't touching that coffee table. (*To Farrah and Velvet*) You move it.
Wayne I'll just get Brooke here into the picture.

Wayne drags Brooke to the front of the sofa. Brooke cries out in pain

Now don't make such a fuss, Brooke — there see, she looks great lying on the floor there, don't she? Like some kind of wounded swan or something.
Velvet She's dying.

Velvet puts her jacket or a coat over Brooke

Wayne We're all dying darlin' from the day we're born. What I'm saying is that her pathetic condition kind of underlines the point I'm making here. So get that coat off her, sugar, it ain't cold and it's spoiling my picture. Ain't nothing sexy 'bout a coat.

Velvet takes the coat off Brooke

Kirsten Mr Hudson.

Wayne Yeah?

Kirsten May I place this boom mike here?

Wayne Sure you can ma'am — OK, this thing's really coming together now. So how about you, what can we do with you?

Wayne looks at Farrah

Farrah What do you mean?

Wayne This is TV, honey, good look'n' woman like you's gonna be a big draw, particularly 'long side of your cute li'l daughter — Scout baby, take Mrs Delamitri and Miss Delamitri and 'cuff them to them pillars up yonder.

Scout Sure will, Buffalo Bill.

Wayne C'mon, get over there girls, we ain't making *Gone With the Wind* here, this is live action...

Scout gets some handcuffs from Wayne's bag. Scout manacles Farrah and Velvet to the pillars

Excuse me partner, would it be OK if I took a look through the lens?

Bill You're the director, sir.

Wayne Well that's right, I guess I am.

Wayne struts over and looks through the lens

OK now, Bruce'll be in the middle, Scout — now you sure you're going to be able to get all this in, Bill? What is your "edge of frame"...

Scout "Edge of frame", did you hear that? "Edge of frame". Wayne you are so cool.

Wayne I know baby, I know.

Bill We have plenty of width. I've just locked it off, we'll take the whole thing in a static six shot, sir. Have another look, sir.

Wayne I don't know, there just seems to be a certain someth'n' missing.

Wayne crosses to Velvet. He studies her for a moment and then rips open Velvet's top

Scout Wayne, take your hands off that girl right now!

Wayne You want the ratings honey? Huh? You want people to watch this thing? Sex is important on TV, sex sells.

Wayne pulls at Velvet's blouse, exposing her shoulders

Cute huh? Can't show too much, of course, there's strict rules. Just enough for the couch potatoes out there in TV land to get themselves off on...

Farrah Don't be scared honey — you look great.

Wayne OK, I guess we're just about ready — so you get up there, Bruce, and get ready to tell America what I said to tell them.

Bruce has been thinking hard, desperately looking for a way out

Bruce Wayne, this isn't going to work. All it will do is screw my life up forever...

Wayne Well, that's a shame Bruce, because it's the best shot I've got and we're going to try it...

Farrah Just do it, Bruce.

Velvet Yes, Daddy, just do it.

Brooke Yeah, do it.

Bruce I'm doing it, for God's sake! I just think there's a better way here Wayne, better for you as well as me.

Wayne Well, if there is, Bruce, I'd be pleased to hear it but I have to tell you that me 'n' Scout have considered every option.

Bruce I think you should debate me.

Wayne Debate you?

Bruce You're not stupid, Wayne, and neither is Scout. You know that the best you have here is a long shot. You know that me claiming responsibility for your actions while you hold a gun to my daughter's head, is not really going to cut a lot of ice. So debate me.

Scout You be careful, Wayne.

Bruce Come on, Scout, remember that stuff you were saying earlier. About me exploiting the ugly and the downtrodden, how I get rich leeching off the suffering of the poor.

Wayne D'you say that, baby doll?

Scout Yes, I did, and I meant it and so did the guy I saw saying it on "Sixty Minutes".

Bruce Well that's a better argument than just using me as some kind of puppet. Put your case. Establish my guilt and let me deny it.

Scout Don't do it darling, your plan's better; just make him say the stuff you said.

Bruce Think of your image, Scout. What do you want that camera to see? A couple of sullen thugs or good-looking, in your face, anti-heroes. By tomorrow morning, you'll be on a million T-shirts, you'll be able to name your price. You'll be stars.

Scout Seems to me we're already stars.

Kirsten has her earphones on

Kirsten Uhm — boss, they want to know what's going on, are we going to give them some pictures or not?

Bruce Come on, Wayne. Or maybe you don't have the balls.

Wayne Oh, I've got the balls, Bruce. I got all the balls, including yours.

Wayne grabs Bruce's balls viciously. Bruce yelps in agony

I don't like being goaded, Bruce. Don't ever think you can goad me — but OK, let's do it. Let's have us a debate.

Wayne releases Bruce. Kirsten speaks into her radio

Kirsten Vision control, stand by, we're going to give you pictures.

Bruce (*in pain*) And then will you let Farrah and Velvet go? Will you let Brooke get to a doctor?

Wayne I never know what I'll do, Bruce — it's my job, I'm a maniac.

Kirsten They're ready in vision control…

Scout Oh Wayne, I look a sight. Can't they send someone in from make-up?

Wayne You look gorgeous, baby.

Scout I do not.

Wayne Brooke did your hair just peachy. Sit down. OK, are you ready, Bruce?

Bruce I still have some discomfort.

Wayne Well that's showbiz. Ya gotta suffer for it. OK Kirsten.

Kirsten OK, we are going to take this thing in *five*, four, three, two, one. And we are live across America.

Wayne No offence, but I think I'll just check we ain't talking to ourselves…

Wayne points the remote at the TV… Clearly they can see that they are on it. We hear Wayne's next speech with an echo on it as because it's also coming out of the TV

That's us honey! We're on TV! We're on TV!

Scout screams

OK, I'll just mute the sound here…

Wayne and Scout are somewhat transfixed by the TV. They experiment with moving their arms. After a moment Bruce clears his throat. Wayne remembers the job at hand

Right, OK, here we are, uhm, Bruce it's your house, maybe you'd better say hi.

Bruce All right Wayne. I will. (*To the camera*) Hallo everybody. I am sorry to interrupt your morning viewing but I guess you all know what's going on here. I'm Bruce Delamitri, the Oscar-winning film maker. The two women you see manacled behind me are Farrah, my wife and our daughter Velvet.

Velvet Please, *Dad*.

Bruce The wounded woman on the floor is Brooke Daniels, the model...

A croak from Brooke

I'm sorry, actress. We are all prisoners of Wayne Hudson, whom you see here, and his partner, Scout.

Wayne Howdy y'all.

Scout Hallo America.

Bruce So let us come to the point. I make films in which actors and stunt artists pretend to kill people. Wayne and Scout actually kill people. They are of course the notorious Mall Murderers and they claim that I am responsible for their actions, that my work has somehow inspired them.

Scout We never said you'd inspired us Mr Delamitri, now don't you go putting words into our mouths.

Wayne Yeah, it ain't like we saw a guy and a girl shooting people in your movie and said "Hell, I never thought of that, that's what we should be doing."

Bruce So my work doesn't inspire you? (*To the camera*) You hear that America, it doesn't inspire them! — Well forgive me Wayne but I can't imagine what other point you're making when you equate me with your disgusting and sickening crimes.

Wayne It ain't a direct thing, Bruce! We ain't morons! We didn't walk straight out of "Ordinary Americans" and shoot the popcorn seller...

Scout Actually we did, Wayne.

Wayne Once! That's all, we did that once! I must have seen that movie fifty times, and only once did we walk out and shoot the popcorn seller.

Wayne Besides which nobody shoots a popcorn seller in "Ordinary Americans"? Do they Bruce?

Bruce I don't believe so.

Wayne You don't believe damn right. Fifty-seven people get shot in "Ordinary Americans".

Scout Wayne counted them.

Wayne Of course I counted them, honey pie, or how would I know? They don't put it up on the titles do they? Like that damn movie you liked — "Marrying and Dying"...

Scout *Four Weddings and a Funeral*. I loved that movie. It must be so great to be English, everything's so elegant and nice.

Wayne Yeah, well, Bruce here did not call his movie "Fifty-seven Murders plus People Taking Drugs and Fucking" did he, the point is ——

Scout Wayne you can't use the F word on live TV.

Kirsten That's OK, they're using a beeper.

Bruce The point is, Wayne, as you yourself have observed, no popcorn seller gets shot in my movie. There's no damn cause and effect here. You see my stuff but you do your stuff, end of story. You'd have killed that guy if you'd just walked out of *Mary Poppins*!

Wayne I guess I probably would at that.

Bruce Of course you would! You are your own man, aren't you? Are you a man, Wayne?

Wayne Of course I'm a man!

Bruce And you do what you want!

Wayne Yes I do.

Bruce Nobody pushes you around, not cops, not hoods and certainly not any damn movie!

Wayne Bruce, I see what you're getting at but you're twisting this thing all around.

Bruce No, I am not.

Wayne Yes, you are.

Scout I don't like this debate! You make him say what you planned, Wayne! Make him read out that newspaper stuff.

Wayne There ain't nothing specific here, I am talking generally.

Bruce Oh generally! Well that's very convenient isn't it. (*To the camera*) You hear that! (*Back to Wayne*) Pretty much covers every eventuality doesn't it? You've screwed up and you feel somehow or other, generally speaking, someone else should take the blame. Me! Society! Who cares, it doesn't matter as long as it isn't you. Now where did I hear that before? Maybe from every failure there ever was. Isn't it funny how nobody ever seems to give society the credit when they succeed!

Wayne Tell me something, Bruce, I've always wanted to know. Do you get a hard-on when you make your movies?

Bruce That is such a cheap shot.

Wayne 'Cos I admit it, that stuff just thrills me — and I look round the movie theatre and I can see all the other guys and they're just loving it. Everyone of them is just itching to haul out a gun and blast away. Of course they don't do it but I can see them licking their lips just the same. It's beautiful, you make killing cool.

Bruce No, Wayne. I make going to the movies cool.

Wayne *Exactly*! I'm talking about a culture that (*he checks one of the newspapers; reading*) "celebrates and exploits violence". We're all livin' it, breathin' it, getting off on it every day and it ain't only the criminals who create it.

Bruce It's only the criminals who commit the crimes! Violent people create a violent society. They do it, not me, not anyone else. They are to blame. You are to blame and you alone!

Scout Now are you sure about that, Mr Big Shot Director?

Velvet Yes, are you sure, Daddy?

Farrah Velvet keep out of this and don't slouch!

Scout Are you sure? Are you sure that no matter how many times you show a sexy murder to a rock and roll soundtrack you ain't eventually going to get into peoples' brains?

Bruce I don't know! I don't know the answer to that! I cannot and will not attempt to second guess the unknowable reactions of criminally insane maniacs! Does *Hamlet* encourage regicide? Does *Oedipus* make people sleep with their mothers?

Scout (*shocked*) Well there is no call for that type of talk!

Bruce (*to the camera*) Cars kill people, you going to ban cars! Booze kills people, maybe we should all sue Jack Daniels! Do movies kill? Probably not, but let's ban them anyway. Then we can put all the directors in prison for murder and the murderers can go on Oprah and tell us how Hollywood made them dysfunctional!

Wayne Fifty-seven murders Bruce, you ever hear of a little boy named Pavlov and his dog.

Kirsten looks up from her screen

Kirsten Excuse me — uhm, this is all very interesting of course, and the producers are delighted, they're *very* happy in control — but I can see here from my ratings monitor that the main channels are losing viewers. They want to know in control whether it would be OK to record this and edit it for the evening news.

Wayne No! I have an idea.

Wayne shouts into the camera

Hey America! Listen, phone your friends, tell them to tune in, because in sixty seconds I'm going to shoot Farrah Delamitri, in sixty seconds she will be one dead mutha!

Farrah No!!

Everybody screams and protests

Bruce Wayne!

Velvet Please, she's my mom!

Bruce How can more killing possibly help your case?

Wayne How are the ratings Kirsten?

Kirsten Yep, they've leapt, but my producer is saying don't kill the woman.

Wayne Is that what he's saying? Well I don't notice him turning off his cameras.

Kirsten He says he has no right to censor the news.

Wayne Well, that's pretty fucking convenient, particularly since we're making the news for his benefit!

Bruce Turn off the broadcast! Turn off the broadcast, turn it off…

Wayne Scout, get him out of the way. Hurry up now y'all. You don't want to miss it do ya? — Five four three two one!

Wayne shoots Farrah. She falls dead, still chained to the pillar

Bruce You bastard! When will this end?

Wayne You saw the ratings, man.

Bruce You hypocritical swine! *You* killed her, no-one else! What is it you're saying? That the media, the public is responsible for the fact that you're a murdering lunatic?

Wayne I'm just saying I wouldn't 'a shot her if people hadn't turned over to another channel. That's all. You work it out.

Bruce You are responsible!

Wayne Yes! I am responsible for me, but you are responsible for you and they are responsible for them. I don't see anyone doing much about that. I've got an excuse, I'm a psycho, what's your get-out?

Kirsten receives a message from the producer. She turns to Bill

Kirsten Bill, get down!

Bill What?

Kirsten The police are coming in!

Kirsten and Bill dive down. Wayne shouts into the camera

Wayne No! Wait! Hold it. I'll give myself up, Scout too! I swear! Stop the attack, Bill, Bill, Bill is this camera rolling?

Bill Yes sir.

Wayne We'll give up! But we give ourselves up to the people. The people are responsible. They decide our fate, the fate of everybody in this room.

Wayne has pushed Scout to the ratings monitor to grab. She does so and hands it to him. Wayne puts it by Brooke's head

It's up to you, the people out there — the lives of us all are in your hands.

Here's how it is. When I've finished talking, if everybody watching switches off their TV, I swear me and Scout will walk out of here with our hands up — But if you keep on watching, I will kill every last mutha in this room, including myself and Scout. Not a bad show huh? Exciting, right? And to see it, all you have to do is stay tuned for another few seconds — well, you're responsible, are you gonna turn off your TV?

Black-out

When ready bring up general lighting

The cast assemble on stage and take their bows

After a decent Curtain call but before the applause has died some sort of change of lighting state occurs. Perhaps a red wash and a spotlight on Bruce. Something to tell the audience, who had been about to leave, that there is something else. The actors tell their stories, remaining in character

Bruce Bruce Delamitri survived Wayne's bloody TV show but his career never recovered. He now makes tired, cynical movies in France. He has written a book about the night Wayne and Scout entered his life, called "I Am Not Responsible".

Brooke Brooke died of her wounds. Her parents claim that by pursuing his debate Bruce denied Brooke the medical care that could have saved her. They are suing him.

Kirsten Bill and Kirsten both died in the police assault. Their families are suing the television companies, whom they claim had a duty of care to their employees.

Bill They are also suing the police whom they claim should have intervened earlier.

Kirsten In a separate claim they are suing the police for intervening at all.

Velvet Velvet was also killed in the crossfire. In the largest single claim in history her grandparents are suing the people who did not turn off their TVs.

Karl The people who did not turn off their TVs have experienced stress and mental torment as a result of the terrible moral dilemma that the TV companies allowed them to be put in. They have formed themselves into action groups and are pursuing claims for damages.

Farrah The TV companies claim that in the final analysis only government can be responsible for how public amenities operate. They are looking to Washington to underwrite their losses.

Wayne Wayne Hudson died in the gun battle with the police. His parents are pursuing the Social Services Department claiming that it was their early neglect that was responsible for turning Wayne bad. Scout's parents are also suing the Social Services claiming that their early intervention made Scout what she was.

Scout Scout survived the gun fight and was eventually sent to a secure mental hospital where she has discovered religion. She feels that the Almighty does all things for a purpose and that in the long run God is responsible for everything.

Bruce So far no-one has claimed responsibility.

Black-out

FURNITURE AND PROPERTY LIST

Further dressing may be added at the director's discretion

ACT I

SCENE 1

On stage: Glass coffee table. *On it*: ashtray
TV/video with remote control
Two sofas with furry cushions
Velvet's magazine
Drinks cabinet. *In it*: bourbon, crème de menthe, bottles, glasses, napkins
Stereo
Rug
Intercom phone
Telephone
Paper and pen
Remote control to operate shutters

Personal: Mobile phone (**Karl**)

SCENE 2

Personal: Machine gun (**Wayne**)
Machine gun (**Scout**)
Bullet belt, with handgun (**Scout**)
Bullet belt. *In it*: knife, pistol containing removable bullets (**Wayne**)

SCENE 3

Off stage: **Bruce**'s podium (**Stage Management**)
Oscar (**Bruce**)

SCENE 4

Off stage: Bag. *In it*: severed ear, "head", bundle of bloodstained magazines and newspapers, two pairs of handcuffs (**Wayne**)

Personal: Bag. *In it*: cocaine, razor blade, gun, comb, hair mousse, tissue (**Brooke**)
Blood capsule (**Brooke**)

ACT II

Off stage: Camera equipment (boom microphone, earphones, radio, ratings
                   moniter etc.) (**Bill** and **Kirsten**)

Samuel French is grateful to Charles Vance, Vice-Chairman of
the Theatres Advisory Council, for the following information
regarding the Firearms (Amendment) Bill:

"The Firearms (Amendment) Bill does not affect blank-firing
pistols which are not readily convertible (i.e. those which do not
require a Firearms Certificate). Among the reasons against
imposing restrictions on such items is their use in theatre, cinema
and television as a "safe" alternative to real guns."

"The general prohibition on the possession of real handguns will
apply to those used for theatrical purposes. It would clearly be
anomalous to prohibit the use of those items for target shooting,
but permit their use for purposes where a fully-working gun is not
needed. As handguns will become 'Section 5' prohibited weapons, they would fall under the same arrangements as at present
apply to real machine guns. As you will know, there are companies which are authorised by the Secretary of State to supply such
weapons for theatrical purposes."

"The exemption under Section 12 of the Firearms Act 1968,
whereby actors can use firearms without themselves having a
Firearm Certificate, will remain in force."

Regulations apply to United Kingdom only. Producers in other
countries should refer to appropriate legislation.

LIGHTING PLOT

ACT I

To open:	Overall general lighting	
Cue 1	**Karl** picks up a phone *Black-out*	(Page 5)
Cue 2	**Wayne** and **Scout** appear *Dim lighting on* **Wayne** *and* **Scout**	(Page 5)
Cue 3	**Scout**: "Oh Wayne, I surely do love you." *Black-out*	(Page 6)
Cue 4	To open scene 3 *Bring up spotlight on* **Bruce**	(Page 6)
Cue 5	**Bruce**: "Thank you." *Cut spotlight*	(Page 6)
Cue 6	**Wayne** and **Scout** enter *Begin gradual fade to general lighting*	(Page 7)
Cue 7	Buzzer sound *Pause. Then black-out*	(Page 25)

ACT II

Cue 8	**Scout** pulls back the drapes *Effect of lights streaming through patio doors etc. as p.33*	(Page 33)
Cue 9	**Wayne**: "… turn off your TV?" *Black-out*	(Page 51)
Cue 10	When ready *Bring up general lighting. When ready change lighting*	(Page 51)
Cue 11	**Wayne**: "… has claimed responsibility." *Black-out*	(Page 52)

EFFECTS PLOT

ACT I

To open: Sound of film clip with music. When ready snap off

Cue 1   **Wayne** (*off*): "You are one dead mutha!"   (Page 5)
           Sound of gun fire and screams

Cue 2   **Wayne**: "No problem, baby doll."   (Page 6)
           Sound of machine gun firing. Screams and sobs. When ready
           cut gunfire. Screaming subsides to a few sobs and fades

Cue 3   **Bruce**: "Thank you."   (Page 6)
           Huge applause

Cue 4   **Bruce** turns the stereo on   (Page 10)
           Snap on stereo music

Cue 5   **Brooke** switches off music   (Page 12)
           Cut stereo music

Cue 6   **Wayne**: "… kept on wasting people."   (Page 20)
           Buzzer sounds

Cue 7   **Wayne**: "… inside of two seconds."   (Page 20)
           Buzzer goes again

Cue 8   **Bruce**: "… out of context."   (Page 20)
           Buzzer goes again

Cue 9   **Wayne**: "… suspicious about nothing."   (Page 20)
           Buzzer goes again

Cue 10   **Wayne**: "… then she can go."   (Page 20)
           Buzzer goes again

Cue 11   **Wayne** takes out his gun   (Page 25)
           Gunshot

Cue 12   **Brooke**: "I'm sorry!"   (Page 25)
           Buzzer sound. Pause

Cue 13	Black-out *Buzzer sound*	(Page 25)

ACT II

To open:	Buzzer sound	
Cue 14	**Wayne**: "… talking and shoot." *Gunshot*	(Page 32)
Cue 15	**Farrah**: "What is going on?" *Sound of helicopter, gradually increasing*	(Page 32)
Cue 16	**Bruce**: "Who is coming to save you?" *Helicopter noise gets louder*	(Page 32)
Cue 17	**Scout**: "… I surely do love you …" *Helicopter sequence as on p.33*	(Page 33)
Cue 18	**Wayne** turns the TV on *Sound of news reporter as on pp.33-34*	(Page 33)
Cue 19	**Wayne**: "… used to ignoring cops." *Phone rings*	(Page 34)
Cue 20	**Wayne**: "… reap a whirlwind." *Phone rings*	(Page 40)
Cue 21	**Wayne** points the remote at the TV *Echo effect from the TV*	(Page 46)
Cue 22	**Wayne**: "OK, I'll just mute the sound here …" *Cut echo effect*	(Page 46)
Cue 23	**Wayne** aims his gun at **Farrah** *Gunshot*	(Page 50)

A licence issued by Samuel French Ltd to perform this play does not include permission to use the Incidental music specified in this copy. Where the place of performance is already licensed by the PERFORMING RIGHT SOCIETY a return of the music used must be made to them. If the place of performance is not so licensed then application should be made to the Performing Right Society, 29 Berners Street, London W1.

A separate and additional licence from PHONOGRAPHIC PERFORMANCES LTD, 1 Upper James Street, London W1R 3HG is needed whenever commercial recordings are used.